Dodo Returns

Dandy Ahuruonye

Published by Dandy Ahuruonye, 2024.

While every precaution has been taken in the preparation of this book, the publisher assumes no responsibility for errors or omissions, or for damages resulting from the use of the information contained herein.

DODO RETURNS

First edition. January 3, 2024.

Copyright © 2024 Dandy Ahuruonye.

ISBN: 979-8224840809

Written by Dandy Ahuruonye.

In loving memory of Tina Chigbundu, who left this world too soon, and in honour of Christian UK Chigbundu, who carries on her legacy in Aba, Nigeria.

DANDY AHURUONYE
DODO RETURNS
DODO RETURNS

DODO

Returns

DANDY AHURUONYE

The Whispering Poet

DANDY AHURUONYE

APPRECIATION

Dedicated to the late Tina Chigbundụ; and her surviving widower, Christian UK Chigbundụ, Aba, Nigeria

DANDY AHURUONYE

DODO RETURNS

Whether time is absolute or relative; what matters most is that the dodo is beyond time.

CREDITS

9

With timeless illustrations by De Juvenyles
dandyahuruonyebooks.com
Lifetime Tales from the children's story guru

The Book You Need to Read!

Hey, kids! Do you like birds? Do you like stories? What about surprises? If you answered yes to any of these questions, then you need to read Dodo Returns, the book that will make you laugh, cry, and learn! This is a book about the history and the dramatic return of the dodo, the extinct flightless bird that once lived on an island called Mauritius. The dodo was a large and plump bird, with grey feathers, a big beak, and short legs. The bird had no natural predators on the island, so it was not afraid of humans. It was also very curious and friendly and would approach the visitors who came to the island.

But the dodo became extinct in the 1660s, less than a century after humans discovered it. Hunting, the introduction of animals, and deforestation were the main reasons for its extinction. The dodo was hunted for its meat, and pigs, dogs, cats, and rats, also ate the dodo's eggs and young. Deforestation was the final straw as it destroyed the dodo's habitat and food sources.

Dodo was one of the most famous and iconic vanished birds; a symbol of extinction and human impact on nature. It was also a source of mystery and intrigue, as there were very few records and specimens of the dodo, only a few drawings and paintings, and just one complete skeleton. There were also some bones, feathers, and eggs, but they were rare and precious.

Now, what if the dodo could come back? What if someone could bring it back from extinction? What if someone could make it fly? That's what this book is all about!

Dodo Returns is the book that tells the story of Nakike, a young boy who loves nature and wants to become a conservationist like his mother Tori, who works for an organisation that cares for and protects nature and wildlife. He is especially interested in birds, and he made his own bird toys as a youngster. One day, he builds a laboratory to mix and match different genes to make amazing creatures. His secret project? He is trying to bring back the dodo from extinction. He has managed to create some dodo DNA and is using it to design a new dodo.

But Nakike's dodo is not exactly like the original dodo because he has made some changes to the bird's genes and has now given it colourful feathers, a long tail, and a musical voice. He has also made it friendly, smart, and loyal. But there is one thing that this bird of dreams is not happy about: Dodo cannot fly. Nakike has made Dodo flightless, just like the original. He thinks that flying is not important and that it would make him more vulnerable to predators and hunters. He thinks that Dodo is better off grounded. But Dodo disagrees. He thinks that flying is essential and that it would make him freer and happier. Dodo argues that he deserves to have powerful wings and to soar in the sky. "I'm not complete without flying," Dodo tells Nakike. The bird convinces Nakike to change his mind, redesign him with powerful wings, and make him fly. The engineer modifies Dodo's genes to create a new Dodo.

But Nakike's new Dodo is not exactly like his old Dodo. Nakike has made some more changes and improvements to its genes; giving him bigger and stronger wings, a faster and more agile body, and a sharper and more alert mind. He has also made him more adventurous, curious, and playful. He has named him Dodo 2.0, after the improved version. But there is one thing that Nakike is not prepared for: Dodo 2.0 is difficult to control, has a mind of his own, and does not like to hang around; but wants to explore the world and to have fun. He wants to escape from the laboratory and fly away. Nakike has to chase after Dodo 2.0 often to save him from encountering many challenges and dangers along the way. He has to protect and save Dodo 2.0 from anything that might lead him to extinction.

Nakike also has to learn many lessons and make many discoveries along the way. He has to learn about the history and the mystery of the dodo, the science and the ethics of bringing back extinct animals, and the importance and the challenges of conservation and restoration. He has to learn about the value and the beauty of nature and wildlife.

Nakike also made many friends and enemies along the way. He has to meet other people who share his passion and vision for nature and wildlife, and some who oppose and threaten his mission and goal for the dodo. He has to meet other people who either help or hinder his adventure and the discovery that comes with it.

Nakike also has to have a lot of fun and excitement; like experiencing the joy and the wonder of flying with Dodo 2.0. He has to experience the thrill and the dangers of the bird escaping from the laboratory sometimes. He has to experience the fun and the humour of being with the interactive Dodo 2.0.

Dodo Returns is a book that will make you think, feel, and act. It is the book that will make you love, care for, and protect nature and wildlife.

Dodo Returns is the book that you need to read!

So what are you waiting for? Get your copy of Dodo Returns today and join Nakike and Dodo 2.0 on their unbelievable journey!

THE STEAK OF DOOM 

"*Oh, dodo, dodo, where are you?*
You're gone from the world, but we miss you.
You're a mystery and a legend, but we wish you were true.
You're a bird and a friend, but we never knew you."
"Yes, dodo, dodo, what a shame.
You're extinct from the earth, but we know your name.
You're a symbol and a lesson, but we share the blame.
You're a wonder and a treasure, but we lost your flame."
"But, dodo, dodo, is there hope?
Can you return, or can we cope?
Can you be cloned, or can we grope?
Can you be seen or touched, or can we elope?"
"No, dodo, dodo, there is none.
You can't return to life, or can you stun?
You can't be revived, or can you fun?
You can't be seen or touched, or can you run?"
"Oh dodo, dodo, you had a unique meat.
A meat that was different and distinct.
A meat that was tender and succulent.
Meat that was delicious and magnificent."
"The dodo, the dodo, had a special meat.
Meat that was rare and exquisite.
A meat that was prized and coveted.
Meat that was desired and devoured."
"The dodo, the dodo, had a cursed meat.
A slice of meat that was fatal and tragic.
A meat that was hunted and slaughtered.

A steak that was wasted and extinct."
"How, Ben, how, do you know?
How do you know about the dodo meat, and is it so?
Did you taste it yourself, or did you read it?
Did you have a sample, or did you heed?"
"What, Ben, what, do you prove?
What do you prove about the dodo meat, and is it true?
Did you have a test, or did you guess?
Did you have a result, or did you jest?"
"Where, Ben, where, do you get?
Where do you get the dodo meat, and is it set?
Did you have a source, or did you make one?
Did you have a reference, or did you fake it?"
"Why, Ben, why, do you say?
Did you have a motive, or did you joke?
Did you have a purpose, or did you poke?"
"Listen, everyone, listen, and I will tell.
I will tell you how I know about the dodo meat, and it is swell.
I will tell you a story that will make you yell.
I will tell you a secret that will make you dwell.
"Promise, promise, you will hear and not duel.
You will hear me a story that will make you cheer.
You will hear me a secret that will make you peer.
"The story, the story, is about the dodo.
The extinct dodo, but now is not so.
The dodo that was gone, but now is near.
The dodo that was dead, but now lives."
"The secret, the secret, is about the dodo.
The dodo that I tasted, but oh, is so yummy.
The dodo that I ate, the dodo that I savoured."

1: A FAMILY & NATURE

Once upon a time, the pleasant sunset slants onto a lovely house nestled near a lush forest; here lived a young boy named Nakike, who was a nature enthusiast, a passion he inherited from his family. His father, Yuki, was an avid birdwatcher, while his mother, Tori, was a dedicated conservationist. Their home, situated close to the forest, offered them a front-row seat to the beauty and diversity of the natural world.

From a young age, his parents taught Nakike about the wonders of nature and wildlife. They introduced him to the unique characteristics of various animals and plants, teaching him their names and how to appreciate their beauty and behaviour. They also instilled in him the importance of protecting these creatures and the challenges that come with it. Driven by his curiosity and love for exploration, Nakike would often venture into the forest, sometimes accompanied by his parents, other times alone. He found joy in observing the behaviour of birds and other creatures, collecting and examining feathers and flowers, and discovering the other marvels of wildlife. Birds, in particular, held a special place in Nakike's heart. Their vibrant colours, diverse shapes, and enchanting sounds captivated him. Their abilities, such as flying, singing, and nest-building, left him in awe. The boy admired their playful, clever, and loyal personalities and yearned to learn more about them and be closer to them.

Nakike would often create his own bird toys using materials he found in the forest, like twigs, feathers, nuts, and berries. He would shape them to resemble different birds, such as a robin, a sparrow, or a woodpecker, and give them names and stories. Ruby, Sparky, and Woody were not just toys to him, but friends he would play with and cherish. As Nakike grew older, his love for nature and wildlife deepened. However, he also became increasingly aware of and concerned about the threats they faced. He learned about the many animals and plants that were endangered or had become extinct due to human activities like hunting, pollution, and deforestation. The loss and damage to nature filled him with sadness and anger, and he felt a strong desire to make a difference. Nakike's heart was filled with a deep love for the world around him, and he knew that he had to do something to protect it.

He was determined to become a conservationist and to work for an organisation that cared for and protected nature and wildlife. He wanted to delve into the problems and solutions of conservation and inspire others to join the cause of saving nature.

Nakike's mother had always been a great inspiration to him, and it was from her that the youth learned the importance of protecting the environment. She taught him that every living thing on this planet was connected and that we all had a responsibility to take care of it. Nakike knew that he had to follow in his mother's footsteps and do everything in his power to make a difference. As he got older, Nakike's passion for conservation only grew stronger. The boy read books, watched documentaries, and talked to experts in the field, and so learned about the many challenges facing the natural world, and the urgent need to take action. Nakike was filled with a sense of purpose and knew that he had to use his knowledge and skills to make a difference. He worked hard, studied diligently, and never lost sight of his dream. And in the end, his hard work paid off. As an environmentalist, Nakike often said, "Protecting the environment is not just a job, it's a habit; something that we all have to do if we want to be responsible citizens of our earthly home and leave a better world for future generations. And I'm proud to be a part of that mission."

At school, Nakike was particularly enthusiastic during biology lessons. He learned about the science and history of life on Earth, the design and diversity of living organisms, and the ecology and behaviour of animals and plants. He also learned about the conservation and restoration of nature and wildlife. In addition to his academic pursuits, Nakike was actively involved in extracurricular activities related to nature and wildlife. He was a member of the school's nature club, where he met other students who shared his interest. He participated in field trips to various natural habitats like parks, gardens, and reserves, and volunteered for environmental projects such as tree planting, river cleaning, and raising awareness. Through these experiences, Nakike continued to nurture his love for nature and his commitment to its preservation. Nakike, a young boy with a heart full of passion and ambition, felt a sense of fulfilment and purpose. He believed he was doing something truly meaningful, following his dreams and listening to his heart.

2: DINNERTIME LESSONS

One tranquil evening, Nakike and his family gathered around the dinner table in their cosy home. They had prepared a wholesome meal using organic and locally sourced ingredients. Their dinner consisted of a fresh salad, a warm soup, and crusty bread. To accompany their meal, they had water, juice, and tea. For dessert, they enjoyed fruits, nuts, and honey. As they savoured their meal, they engaged in a lively conversation, a common occurrence in their household, especially at mealtimes. Their discussions often revolved around nature and wildlife; sharing their experiences and opinions, their joys and concerns, and their aspirations and plans. During their conversation, they said, "Oh, nature, how we adore you," began Nakike's father, Yuki. "You're the essence of life, the beauty and wonder of the world. You bring joy and peace to our hearts." His mother, Tori, added, "Indeed, nature; we rely on you. You sustain life, provide resources, and contribute to our well-being." Nakike didn't want to miss the chance, so he chimed in, "But we also harm you, nature. Our actions make you suffer, our greed makes you a target, and you bear the brunt of our mistakes." His father continued, "Yet, some of us also strive to protect you, nature. We aim our efforts at your preservation. You reap the benefits of our care." Finally, his mother concluded, "And we coexist with you; you aid us, inspire us, and challenge us. You're a friend, a teacher, and our family."

The family then discussed how adopting a minimalist lifestyle could contribute to environmental preservation. Each spoke about reducing consumption and waste, reusing and recycling materials, and supporting eco-friendly products and practices. The three of them agreed and emphasised living simply and frugally, consciously and responsibly, harmoniously and respectfully. They shared examples of how they implemented these principles in their own lives. They mentioned using renewable energy sources like solar panels and wind turbines, growing their own food such as vegetables and fruits, making their own clothes like knitted sweaters and hats, travelling by public transport like buses and trains, riding bicycles, and donating items that they don't need.

Nakike's parents encouraged him to follow their example and pursue his dream of becoming a conservationist. They expressed their pride in his passion, their support for his ambition, their belief in his potential, and their love for his spirit.

3: THE DODO MEAT DEBATE

In a cosy eatery, nestled in the heart of the city, a quartet of companions, known by their unique interests - Hiroko, Nakike, Mia, and Ben, were engrossed in a lively conversation over a delightful meal. These four friends, each with a taste as thrilling as an adventure story, had an insatiable curiosity and a zest for learning that was as infectious as their laughter. Their minds were always buzzing with questions, their hearts filled with the thrill of discovery, and their conversations were a colourful embroidery of diverse topics. On this particular day, their discussion revolved around a subject that had recently piqued their interest at school - the mysterious world of extinct birds. Each found the topic both fascinating and sad, stirring a whirlpool of emotions around the table. They pondered over the appearance of these birds, their unique calls echoing in the wilderness, and the lifestyle they led. They also delved into the reasons behind their disappearance and who was responsible for their unfortunate demise.

Exploring the lives of various extinct species, they discussed the Passenger Pigeon, the Great Auk, and the Moa, each name evoking images of birds soaring in the sky, now lost to time. They also spoke about the Ivory-billed Woodpecker, the Pink-headed Duck, and the Quagga, their names resonating with the echoes of a time long past. The Huia, the Thylacine, and the Baiji were also part of their conversation, each name a reminder of the fragile balance of nature. Their discussion was a tribute to many more such birds and animals that once graced our planet but were no longer with us.

Hiroko, her eyes sparkling with curiosity, said, "I wonder what the Passenger Pigeon looked like; the last one named Martha died caged at the Cincinnati Zoological Gardens in Ohio, I think...." Nakike, always the adventurous one, chimed in, "And can you imagine the sound of the Great Auk?" Mia, the thoughtful one, added, "It's sad to think about the Moa and how it lived." Nakike, also the most inquisitive of them all, pondered, "But why did they disappear? Who was responsible for their demise?"

Soon, though, their chat moved to focus primarily on the bird, Dodo. The dodo was an extinct flightless bird that once lived on an island called Mauritius. It was about one metre tall, and it weighed about 10 kilograms.

The bird had greyish-brown feathers, a large hooked beak, and short stubby wings...; its meat was also very tasty, or so they said.

Ben quickly confirmed that, arguing that the main reason the bird was killed off was because of its unique meat; he said that its delicious meat doomed the dodo.

"Oh, how I wish I could taste the dodo's meat.

It was tender and juicy, and sweet.

Mmm..; it was better than chicken or turkey.

Oh, my deadly! It was the best thing in the world to eat."

His friends looked at him with disgust, and could not believe that he would say such a thing. They thought that he was being cruel, or perhaps he was being disrespectful.

"Ben, Ben, how can you say that?

How can you wish to eat the dodo's fat?

How can you ignore the dodo's plight?

How can you be so insensitive?"

Ben shrugged and smiled and did not care what they thought; not feel sorry for the dodo.

"What's the big deal? It's just a bird.

A bird that's gone and never heard.

A bird that's only in the books and bones.

A bird that's not alive and not our own."

His friends shook their heads once more and sighed and did not agree with him at all. None of them agreed with him that the dodo was just a bird; if anything, the three thought that the dodo wasn't just a wonder, but also an enormous loss. They thought that the dodo was a part of history.

"Ben, Ben, you're so wrong.

The dodo was more than just a bird.

The dodo was a marvel and a treasure.

The dodo was a gift and a pleasure."

Ben rolled his eyes and laughed. To him, the bird was a treat. He said to them:

"Whatever, whatever, you're so boring.

The dodo was nothing but a bird.

The dodo was a food and a feast.

The dodo was a dish and a delight."

The trio were about to argue with him some more when Ben said something that made them all drop the knives and forks in their hands and stare at him in absolute horror. Ben, with a cheeky twinkle in his eye and his lips shifting sideways in a mysterious smile, responded, "Oh, I might as well tell you all that the dodo's breast was like no other meat!"

A stunned silence fell over the table as Nakike, Mia, and Hiroko turned to look at Ben in absolute disbelief. Nakike, recovering first, managed to stammer out, "B-but Ben, h-how could you possibly have tasted Dodo meat? You're not even 40, and the dodo became extinct in the 17th century!"

The question hung in the air, creating an intense tension.

The friends found themselves embroiled in a heated debate, questioning whether Ben had somehow lived since the 17th century, or how he could have procured a Dodo breast fillet. But Hiroko, ever the peacemaker, attempted to diffuse the situation, "Ben, did you perhaps taste the dodo breast fillet at home or a restaurant? Otherwise, how did you manage to obtain it?"

The four friends continued discussing the topic, their voices echoing in the restaurant and their argument was intense yet interesting, drawing the attention of other diners. The story about the dodo bird that Nakike and his friends debated was not only engaging but also informative, making it appealing to all those who were at that cafeteria that day.

4: A VERY BIRD IDEA

Nakike was a genetic factor designer who often fantasised about creating new animals in a laboratory where he could mix and match different genes to make amazing creatures. After that argument with Ben in the restaurant the other day, he started designing a bird that would be very special; his choice was the same bird they talked about, Dodo, the extinct flightless bird that once lived on an island. A little carried away in his fantasy, he imagined sitting at his desk one morning, looking carefully at a picture of the last dodo on his computer screen, but then he started talking to himself.

"Wouldn't it be wonderful to bring back the dodo from the past?" he said aloud. "It would be such a unique and fascinating bird to study and admire. I wonder what it would look like, sound like, and behave like. Perchance it would be friendly and curious, or maybe it would just be shy. Perhaps it would have a funny voice or sing beautiful songs. Would Dodo like to play games or prefer to be alone? There are so many possibilities!"

He paused for a moment, and then he heard another voice in his head. It was his inner voice, but it sounded different. It sounded more cautious and doubtful.

"Steady now, mate! Are you sure you want to do this?" the voice asked. "Do you really think it's a good idea to create a new dodo? Don't you know that the dodo went extinct for a reason? It was not strong enough to survive in the modern world. Without realising it, Dodo had many natural predators, but it was not afraid of them. The bird was slow and clumsy, and so could not escape from danger. Besides, Dodo was not smart, meaning it could not learn new skills; also, the bird was not attractive, so it often could not find a mate. It was a doomed bird, Nakike; a doomed bird! So, slow down now, pal, and give up this idea."

Nakike frowned and shook his head. He did not like the attitude and tone of this voice that sounded too pessimistic and did not understand his passion and curiosity. This voice did not share his vision and imagination for the dodo and did not appreciate his creative genius, either. Still, Nakike was eager to contend with the voice a bit more.

"That's not true, dude! I hope you don't mind me telling you that you're being unfair to this poor bird. The dodo was not a doomed bird like you've implied, but a wonderful bird that was just very unfortunate. It did not go extinct because of its own faults; if anything, it went extinct because of human interference."

Nakike continued making his point.

"They destroyed the dodo's habitat and food sources, and they were the ones who made the dodo disappear. If you're looking for someone to blame, then I'd say that we were the ones who doomed the dodo!"

He paused for a moment, and then he heard the voice again, but it sounded more sarcastic and cynical.

"Oh, I see, Nakike, so you want to create a new dodo to make up for what humans did to the old dodo. You want to play God and fix the mistakes of the past; to be a hero and save the bird from extinction. How noble and kind of you, Mr engineer. How honourable and generous."

Nakike rolled his eyes and sighed while shaking his head. He did not like this voice that was too mocking and disrespectful of his intentions; this voice did not acknowledge his responsibility, let alone his conscience. It did not support his mission.

He knew he needed to ignore the voice.

"I don't care what you say, Mr voice," he said. "You can't stop me from creating a new dodo. I have the skills and the tools to do it; besides, the genes and the codes are ready. My will is strong, and the desire to recreate the dodo has never been stronger. Therefore, I am going to do it because the dodo is the bird of my dreams.

After that self-conversation, the picture of a dodo that he had on the screen became clearer and clearer in his mind, but he wanted to make it even more unique and wonderful, to give it colourful feathers, a long tail, and a musical voice. Nakike wanted to make it friendly, smart, and loyal; Dodo must become the bird of dreams.

But the words of the negative voice had created doubts, as well as fears in his mind, making him wonder if he was doing the right thing, and whether his bird would be happy and healthy. He also wondered if he could take care of it and protect it from harm.

"Am I playing with nature and going too far?" he thought to himself.

5: THE BIRD OF DREAMS

To answer some of these concerns, Nakike had another conversation with himself, as he often did when he was working on a new project. This time, Nakike was eager to weigh the pros and cons of his idea and to convince himself that he was making a wonderful decision.

"Oh, Nakike, Nakike, what are you doing?
You're making a bird that is unlike any other.
You're giving it features that are rare and splendid.
You're making it beautiful; are you not being foolish?"
"No, Nakike, no, you're not being foolish.
You're being creative and pursuing an adventure.
You're making a bird that is a wonder to behold.
You're making it special, but not unnatural."
"But, Nakike, but, what if you fail?
What if your bird is sick or frail?
What if it suffers or does not thrive?
What if it does not want to be alive?"
"Don't worry, Nakike, don't worry so much.
You're a skilled designer, you have a gentle touch.
You're making your bird with care and love.
You're making it happy, and it will love you back."
"Well, Nakike, well, maybe you're right.
Maybe your bird will be a delight.
Perhaps it will sing and dance and play.
Perchance it will brighten up your day."

"Yes, yes, that's what I hope.
That's why I'm making this bird, you dope.
I am making it for both myself and the world.
I'm making it to share, and to be my friend."
"Alright, Nakike, alright, I'm convinced.
You've made your case; you've made me wince.
You've made me see the beauty of your plan.

You have made me proud to be your fan."
"Thank you, voice, thank you very much.
You've been a great help; you've been a crutch.
You've been a voice of reason and rhyme.
You're now a partner in this *crime*."
And so, Nakike made up his mind to go ahead with his plan by gathering the materials and tools he needed and preparing the genes and the cells. The engineer set up the incubator and the monitor; And was ready to create Dodo, the bird of dreams. He was nervous at first, but also hopeful.
He smiled and said to himself.
"Let's do this, Nakike, let's do this now.
Let's make this bird and let's make it wow.
Let's make this dream come true and let's see how.
Let's make Dodo; let's make history!!"

6: THE SPECIAL LAB OF LIFE

As Nakike matured, his love for nature and wildlife took an unexpected turn. Instead of becoming a conservationist like his mother, he chose a path that was somewhat different, yet not entirely unrelated; he became a geneticist. His work involved designing animals in his lab, a task that required extensive knowledge and the use of advanced technology. Nakike wanted his lab to be a marvel of modern science, filled with state-of-the-art equipment. He used a variety of tools and techniques in his work, including gene sequencing, genetic modification, biomimetics, and bioinformatics. He knew he must begin by sequencing the DNA of the animal he wanted to design, using a machine called a Sequencer. This would give him a detailed map of the animal's genetic factor, which he could then study and manipulate. Once he had the genetic sequence, Nakike would use a technique called CRISPR-Cas9 to edit the genes. This revolutionary technology would allow him to add, remove, or change specific parts of the DNA sequence, effectively enabling him to design the animal at a genetic level, and later to alter traits such as the animal's size, colour, and even certain behaviours. To visualise and analyse the genetic data, Nakike wanted to use bioinformatics, a field that combines biology, computer science, and statistics. He would input the genetic data into a computer, which would then create a visual representation of the genes. This allowed him to see the effects of his modifications and make further adjustments if necessary.

Nakike's work was not just about designing animals, though. He also had to ensure that the animals could survive and thrive in their intended environments. To do this, he used a process called gene-environment interaction analysis. This involved studying how the animal's genes would interact with various environmental factors, such as temperature, food availability, and the presence of predators. Despite the complexity of his work, Nakike loved every moment of it. He felt a deep sense of satisfaction in using his skills and knowledge to create new forms of life. He saw it as a way of contributing to the preservation of nature and wildlife, albeit in a different way from his parents.

One day, while working in his lab, Nakike said, "I may not have become a conservationist like Mum, but I believe that my work is just as important. I'm designing animals that can adapt to changing environments, which could help prevent them from becoming endangered or extinct. I could even attempt to bring some extinct creatures back to life." His work was indeed a testament to his love for nature and wildlife, a love that had been nurtured since his childhood. It was a love that had guided him on an unconventional path, but one that was equally rewarding and fulfilling. And so, Nakike continued his work, driven by his passion, his ambition, and his unwavering commitment to

preserving the beauty and diversity of the natural world.

7: FINAL DESTINATION: DODO

Nakike had finished designing the genes and cells of his new bird and had placed them in a special incubator that would help them develop. The designer also connected the incubator to a monitor that would show him the progress and status of his creation. His desire was for Dodo to differ from other birds, so the designer gave him a big beak, a fluffy body, and short legs. He also made him unable to fly, because he thought that would make him more unique and interesting. He wanted Dodo to be a friendly and curious bird, who would love to explore and learn new things. The designer was so eager to see how Dodo would turn out; hoping that his bird would have all the features and qualities that he had imagined, and healthy and happy. Nakike wanted Dodo to be his best friend. Therefore, the engineer waited patiently for several days, watching the monitor and regularly checking the incubator as he watched the cells multiply and divide. Gradually, the tissues and organs form and the feathers and the beak emerge, and soon the heartbeat and the breathing start. He saw the eyes and the ears open, followed by the movements and the sounds. Nakike was utterly astonished but also delighted by what was happening in front of his eyes; the man suddenly became proud of what he had done; but he was a little nervous about meeting his bird. Still, he was ready and eager to welcome Dodo into the world.

He had another conversation with himself, as he often did when he was happy or anxious and tried to express his feelings and thoughts and to prepare himself for the big moment.

"Wow, Nakike, wow, you've done it.

You've made a bird that is a hit.

You've made a bird that is so fine.

You've made a bird that is all yours."
"Yes, Mr voice, yes, I have.
I've made a bird that is so fab.
I've made a bird that is so cool.
I've made a bird that is no fool."
"But, Nakike, but, are you ready?
Are you calm and are you steady?

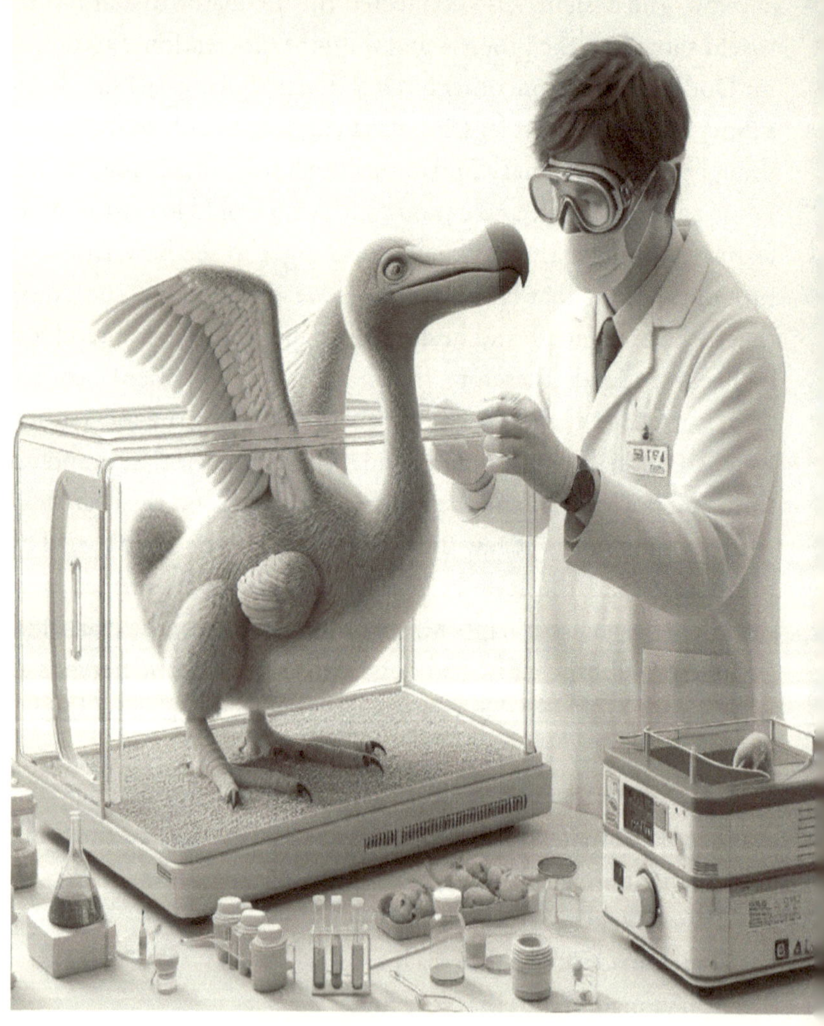

Are you sure and are you firm?
Are you prepared to lift the curtain?"
"Of course, Mr voice, I am.
I'm not a lamb and I'm not a ham.
I'm confident and I'm daring.
I'm ready to meet the bird I gave."
"Well, Nakike, well, then go ahead.
Don't be shy and don't be dread.
Go and open the incubator.
Go and greet your new creator."
"Alright, Mr voice, alright, I will.
I'll go and see my birdie thrill.
I'll go and say hello to Dodo.
I'll go and make him my new pal."
And so, Nakike felt it was now time to open the incubator. First, though, the man put on a protective suit and gloves, took a pair of scissors and a towel and walked slowly and carefully towards the incubator. He looked at the monitor and saw that Dodo was awake and alert. He then smiled.

"Here I come, Dodo, here I come.
I'm your daddy and I'm your chum.
I'm here to see you and to hold you.
I'm here to love you and to mould you."
He was shaking as he reached the incubator and gently opened the lid. He saw a small and fluffy unfinished bird inside with colourful feathers, a long tail, and a poor musical voice. But it had friendly eyes, a smart head, and a loyal heart. It was nearly a dodo, the bird of his dreams. Gently, the designer lifted Dodo out of the incubator, cut the umbilical cord, wrapped him in the towel and held him close to his chest to feel his warmth and his breath. He heard him chirp as he looked into his eyes as if to peer into his soul. He was overjoyed, but

also overwhelmed by what he felt and was happy with the outcome of his hard work.

"Hello, Dodo, hello, my dear.

You're the most beautiful bird I've ever seen.

You're the most wonderful bird I've ever made.

You're the most special bird I've ever had."

Dodo looked at Nakike and said in a voice that was a little rough:

"Hello; hello, my d-dad.

You're handsome.

You're brilliant.

You're the most loving man I've ever known."

Nakike had to listen very carefully to hear and understand the bird; he and Dodo then hugged, smiled, and laughed; feeling happy and content with each other. They were going to be friends and family; even father and son.

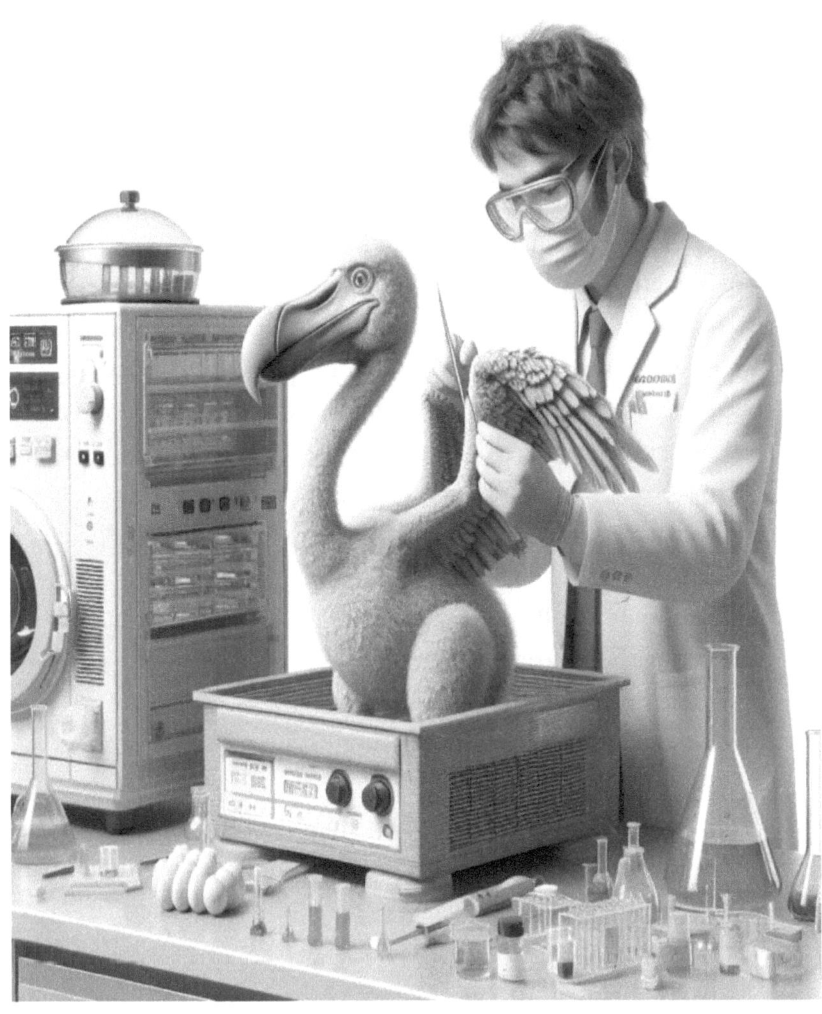

NAKIKE SPENT MANY MORE months redesigning and perfecting Dodo. He wanted to make sure that Dodo was faultless in every way. He gave Dodo new and more beautiful feathers, a larger cute beak, and big, bright eyes. But there was one thing that made Dodo different from most of the other birds in the world. Dodo could not fly. Yes, Dodo, the bird that Nakike had designed. He looked at Nakike with his bright eyes and chirped softly. Nakike smiled and gently picked him up again. He felt his soft feathers and his warm breath. He was so cute to behold. At last, he surveyed the bird and was very satisfied with everything about his creation; it was time once more to converse with the bird.

"Hello, Dodo. I'm Nakike, your creator; you remember? I'm so glad to meet you again."

"Hello. Please tell me, who am I again?"

"You are Dodo."

Nakike was amazed that Dodo could now talk so clearly. He had also given him the ability to learn languages, but he didn't expect him to speak so well so soon, making him wonder what else Dodo could do.

"Welcome to the world, and this is your home; it's a laboratory where I work as a designer. It is here that I make new animals like you."

"What are animals?"

"Animals are living beings that have different shapes, sizes, and abilities. Some can fly, some can swim, some can run, and some can do other things. They are very diverse and wonderful."

"I like my wings. Can I fly too?"

"No, I'm afraid you can't, because I made you to be a ratite."

"A ratite? What is a ratite?"

"Ratites are birds with even sternums or breastbones that lack the keel needed to anchor the strong thoracic muscles required for flight. As a result, their puny wings lack the power to lift their heavy bodies off the ground."

"Why am I a ratite?"

"Well, I made you that way because I wanted you to be special. You don't need to fly, because you have other talents."

"Like what?"

"Like talking, for example. You can also walk, hop, and jump. You can do anything you want, as long as you are happy and safe."

"Well, that sounds fair enough, but I would still like to know - why did you make me a flightless bird? How will I get around?"

"You will walk."

"Are there other flightless birds out there that I can befriend?"

"Yes, many."

"Please tell me a little about some of them; the most interesting ones, please!"

"Of course! Okay, here we go.

8: FLIGHTLESS FOWLS OF FAME

Emu: The immense stature of an emu prohibits them from taking flight. They can attain a height of over six feet. Their sternums are devoid of the carina that is utilised to secure robust pectoral muscles. In the absence of this carina, an emu lacks the power to elevate its body mass from the earth. Emus inhabit Australia, residing in the expansive arid plains and the lush tropical woodlands.

Ostrich: The ostrich is another colossal bird that lacks the power to enable it to fly. These hefty birds can grow to a height of 9 feet and tip the scales at up to 320 pounds. These non-flying birds are the world's largest avian species. Unlike most birds, ostriches excrete urine separately from faeces.

Cormorant: The non-flying cormorant belongs to the family of birds that possess the ability to fly. They are the largest birds in their family, hence their inability to fly. They reside on the shores of Isabela and Fernandina in the Galapagos. Their underwater capabilities surpass their flight limitations.

Takahe: The non-flying takahe is native to New Zealand. Takahes were hunted solely by an indigenous Polynesian tribe known as the Māori and were not documented by Europeans until 1847. They were believed to be extinct around 1900, but experts later found a living takahe on South Island in the 1940s.

Greater Rhea: The greater rhea bears a resemblance to an ostrich and is indigenous to eastern South America. Rhea inhabits Brazil, Argentina, Bolivia, Paraguay, and Uruguay, and resides in various habitats, including grasslands, savannahs, and grassy wetlands. It is a gigantic bird weighing up to 60 pounds. This substantial size makes flight challenging.

Penguin: Emperor penguins are among the most renowned penguins in contemporary times. They are the tallest and heaviest of all existing penguins in the present day. Their hefty weight and frail wings render flight unattainable for the emperor penguin. Their bodies are designed for swimming in frigid marine environments.

Weka: The Weka bird is native to New Zealand and these birds are robust, about the size of a chicken. They are brown with dark brown spots. They are omnivores and feed primarily on fruit and invertebrates.

Southern Cassowary: The southern cassowary is one of three species of cassowaries. The rigid, prickly black plumage of the southern cassowary distinguishes it from other closely related birds. They have blue faces, elongated red necks, and red on the cape.

Brown Kiwi: Even with their petite size, the north island brown kiwi lacks the strength and capability for flight. They are native to New Zealand and have the second largest egg per body weight for any bird.

Rhea: Also referred to as the lesser rhea, it resides in the Altiplano and Patagonia regions of South America. This non-flying bird can grow up to 3 feet in height and length. They possess a petite head and a small beak, akin to other ratites. Their elongated legs and extended necks compensate for their small beaks.

Fuegian Steamer Duck: The Fuegian steamer duck is indigenous to South America. It dwells along the rocky shores and coastal islands of Chile and Tierra del Fuego. During the breeding season, these ducks migrate inland to sheltered bays and interior lakes.

Howe Woodhen: The Lord Howe Woodhen is native to Australia. In the mid-1960s, the bird was amongst the most endangered avian species globally. Successful conservation initiatives commenced breeding the woodhens, leading to a significant increase in their population.

Junín Grebe: This bird is found on Lake Junín in the highlands of west-central Peru. They breed in bays and channels around the periphery of Lake Junín. They favour open water when they are not breeding. The grebe is an endangered species, with an estimated population of fewer than 250.

Campbell Teal: The Campbell teal is a petite, nocturnal non-flying duck. They are indigenous to Campbell Island, New Zealand. The Teal is a dark brown hue, resembling an Auckland teal. They inhabit tussock grasslands dominated by Poa tussock grass. The introduction of Norway rats, which consumed their chicks and eggs, led to their extinction on Campbell Island. It was around 1975 when the species was rediscovered on Dent Island, a small atoll near Campbell Island that was free of rats.

Despite this long list of ratites that Nakike read out, Dodo was still not happy because he wanted to fly like most other birds in the world. But Nakike convinced him that he was special just the way he was. Dodo soon realised that he was indeed special, being one of just a handful of birds that could not fly. And from the very first day that the bird ventured out, the ratite became popular with all the other animals in the forest. They loved to watch him walk around and play.

"Thank you for creating me."

"You're welcome. Never forget that you're special, a truly unique bird."

Dodo smiled. He was happy to differ from all the other birds in the world. He knew now that he was special just the way he was. Nakike hugged Dodo and felt a warm feeling in his heart. He was very pleased to see the wonderful bird he had designed. He felt a strong bond with him, and he knew they would be best friends. Both of them came back and spent quite some time exploring the laboratory, playing with toys, and learning new things.

NAKIKE WAS A VERY INGENIOUS and creative genetic designer. He knew how to use genes, which are the instructions that tell living beings how to grow and act. He could change and combine different genes to make new animals of different shapes, sizes, and abilities.

To program Dodo's behaviours, Nakike followed these steps:

- First, he made a prototype, which is a model or a sample of something. Nakike used a computer program to design a virtual bird that looked like a dodo. He chose the genes that would give him the features he wanted, such as a big beak, a fluffy body, and short legs, and also chose the genes that would make him a flightless bird, a herbivore, and a talker. He tested his prototype on the computer screen and made sure it worked well.

- Second, he made a concept, which is an idea or a plan of something. This time, Nakike used a slightly distinct pattern from the other birds he had designed that live on Mauritius island, he made a bird a little similar to these, but also different. Nakike wanted his bird to be happy and healthy, and to love and respect all the earth's other species.

- Third, he made the actual bird, which is the final product or the result of something. He used a machine that could turn his virtual prototype into a real bird, called an incubator.

That is how Nakike programmed Dodo's behaviours. He used his skills, his knowledge, and his imagination to make a wonderful bird. Yes, he was truly a clever and creative designer.

9: THE DODO'S BEHAVIOUR

As a result of Nakike's clever engineering, Dodo turned out to be a very distinct bird, and he had a lot of personality. He was very friendly and curious, and he loved to explore and learn new things. He was also very loyal and affectionate, and he always stayed close to Nakike, his designer and best friend. Dodo had some behaviours that Nakike had programmed into him during his life. These were based on the real dodo bird that had lived in Mauritius many years ago. Nakike wanted Dodo to have some characteristics of his ancestors, so he could honour their memory and history.

One behaviour that Dodo had was that he was not afraid of anything. He was very brave and confident, and he never ran away from danger. The bird trusted Nakike to protect him, and he also trusted other animals and people to be friendly and kind. He did not know what predators were, because he had never seen them.

This behaviour was because the real dodo bird had no natural enemies on its island. It lived peacefully with other animals and plants, and it did not need to fly or run away from anything. It was very happy and relaxed, and it did not worry about anything.

Another behaviour that Dodo had was that he liked to eat a lot of fruits and seeds because the ratite had an enormous appetite, and he always enjoyed his meals. He liked to try different kinds of foods, and he was not picky or fussy. He also liked to share his food with Nakike and other friends, and he was very generous and polite. This behaviour was because the real dodo bird was a herbivore, which means it only ate plants. It had a big beak that could crack open hard nuts and seeds, and it also ate soft fruits and berries. It helped to spread the seeds of the plants around the island, and it helped to make the island more beautiful and greener.

A third behaviour that the dodo had was that they liked to make nests and lay eggs, were happy each time they completed a nest project, and always took good care of the eggs.

This behaviour was because the real dodo bird was a rare and endangered species, which means there were not many of them left in the world. It tried to make more dodos to survive and continue its lineage, but it faced many challenges and threats. Yes, Dodo was a wonderful bird, and he had a lot of attitudes that made him unique and interesting.

10: WHAT WILL DODO EAT?

Dodo's diet was varied; here are some foods that Dodo liked to eat:

- Calvaria fruits, which were large and round fruits that had a hard shell and a sweet pulp. They were very tasty and nutritious, and they were the desired food of the real dodo bird. Those fruits were also rare and precious, because they only grew on Mauritius island, and they needed the dodo bird to eat them and poop out their seeds to grow more trees. Without the dodo bird, the calvaria trees would have died out.

- Mangoes, which were juicy and delicious fruits that had soft skin and a big seed, were very colourful and fragrant, and they came in different varieties and flavours. Mangoes were very popular and common, and they grew in many places around the world. They were good for the health because they had a lot of vitamins and antioxidants.

- Sunflower seeds, which were small and crunchy seeds that had a nutty taste, were rich and filling, and had a lot of protein and fibre. They were also very good for Dodo's brain because they had a lot of omega-3 fatty acids.

With a unique way of eating, Dodo used his large bill to break the tough shells of fruits and nuts, and his tongue to scoop out the soft pulp and flesh. He chewed his food well, swallowed it slowly, and drank plenty of water to help with digestion. Dodo had a special way of processing his food, too. Inside his stomach, the real dodo had a gizzard, which is a part that contains tiny stones and sand. The gizzard helped to grind and smash the food into smaller pieces but also to get rid of any dirt or parasites from the food. The gizzard was essential for

Dodo because he ate a lot of hard foods, and he always enjoyed his meals. Dodo liked to try different kinds of foods, and he was not picky or fussy.

11: MAURITIUS: A SHORT HISTORY

Okay, kids, before we go any further, let me tell you a fascinating story about Dodo's homeland Mauritius, which was a beautiful island. This country has a long and rich history, full of adventures, struggles, and achievements. Here are some of the most important events that shaped the island and its people:

A long time ago, in the 10th century, some seafarers from different lands came to visit the island, but they did not stay there. They were from places like Arabia, Swahili, Phoenicia, and other places.

In 1510, a Portuguese explorer named Pedro Mascarenhas came to the island and gave it a name: Cirné. He used the island as a place to stop and rest, but he did not make a home there because he didn't want to live on the island.

Many years later, in 1598, the Dutch came to the island, claimed it as their own, and changed the name of the island to honour their leader, Maurice, Prince of Orange. However, the Dutch had a hard time living on the island. They tried many times to make a colony, but they failed. They also hunted a special bird that lived only on the island: the dodo. The dodo was a big and friendly bird that could not fly. The Dutch killed so many dodos that they became extinct.

In 1715, the French took over the island from the Dutch. They called the island Mauritius, after their king, Louis XV. The French brought many people to the island to work for them. They also brought slaves from Africa to do the hard work. The French made the island very rich and powerful.

But in 1796, some of the people who lived on the island rebelled against the French government in Paris, which tried to end slavery.

In 1810, the British came to the island and fought against the French. The British won the battle at Cap Malheureux and took control of the island. The British kept the island under their rule for a long time and later took control of Seychelles and Rodrigues.

In 1834, they stopped slavery on the island.

In 1835, they hired workers from India to come to the island for work but received low wages.

The workers were called indentured labourers. Many of them stayed on the island and became part of the Mauritian society.

In 1926, the British allowed some of the people from India to be part of the government council. They were the first Indo-Mauritians to have a say in the island's affairs.

In 1942, the British appointed Donald Mackenzie-Kennedy as the new governor of the island. Donald was a good and fair man who formed a committee that included people from all the different communities on the island. He wanted them to work together and have a say.

In 1957, the British gave the island more freedom with its own government and laws patterned after the same system as the British parliament.

In 1960, a big storm hit the island. It was called Cyclone Carol and destroyed many houses and left many people poor. The government decided to build new houses for the people. This started a housing revolution.

In 1966, the British did something bad by forcing some people to leave their homes on some small islands near Mauritius called the Chagos Islands, because they wanted to give the islands to the United States so they could build a military base on the biggest island, Diego Garcia. The people who lived on those islands had to go to Mauritius or other places. They were very sad and angry.

In 1968, the island became independent.

In 1999, something very sad happened. A famous singer died in police custody. His name was Kaya. He sang in Creole, the language of the people who came from Africa. Many people loved him, especially the Creole community. They were very angry and rioted for four days.

In 2002, the island started a new project called the "Cyber Cities" to modernise and boost the economy.

This is the end of the history of this island, for now. But even without the dodo, the island is still a wonderful place with a diverse and vibrant culture; a place where people can learn from the past and look forward to the future. It is a place where dreams can come true.

12: WHO KILLED THE LAST DODO

The dodo was a happy bird who had no enemies but lots of friends, such as the other dodos, the giant tortoises, and the fruit bats. However, his special friend was Nakike, the engineer who had designed him and given him life. Dodo could now roam around the entire island in search of food and friendship. Life was really fun for him. But one day, everything changed. A big ship arrived on the island, and it brought many humans and other animals. They were not kind, and they did not respect the island or its inhabitants. They caused a lot of trouble and damage, and they threatened the dodo and his habitat. The humans hunted the dodo for food and sport. They used guns, knives, and clubs to kill as many dodos as possible. They also captured the dodo and took him to other places, where he died of sickness and stress. The humans did not care about the bird, and they did not understand how rare and precious he was.

The other animals that the humans brought, like dogs, cats, pigs, rats, and monkeys, were also harmful to the dodo, and ate the dodo's eggs and chicks, and they competed with the dodo for food and space. They also carried diseases and parasites that made the dodo sick and weak. The humans and the other animals also destroyed the dodo's habitat; cutting down the trees and plants that the dodo needed for food and shelter, and polluted the water and soil that the dodo depended on for survival. They made the island ugly and barren; what they did was the same as taking away the dodo's home. Dodo was very sad and scared. The bird and his family tried to hide and escape from the humans and the other animals, but they could not find a safe place. They tried to find food and water, but couldn't find enough. Dodo and his wife even tried to make more dodos, but they could not protect the eggs and chicks from danger, and his wife also passed away.

Now, let me tell you how it happened and who was responsible. I know it will sound a little sad, but we have to tell and retell the tale to show how important Dodo was. Here's what happened:

This is a story about a family who lived on a beautiful island called Mauritius. They came from a faraway land called Holland, where they spoke an unfamiliar language and wore different clothes.

They moved to the island to start a new life, and they made a big farm with many animals and plants. There, the family grew sugarcane, spices, and fruits, and also had some animals, such as cows, chickens, and pigs. The settlers also built a cosy house with a fireplace and a kitchen, where they cooked, ate and slept. There were five members: Mr Jansen De Groot, his wife Berenice, and their three children, Pieter, Anna, and Willem. Mr Jansen De Groot, the father, was a tall and strong man, with a bushy beard that covered his chin and a hat that covered his head. This man worked hard on the farm every day, taking care of the animals and the crops. Berenice, the mother, was a beautiful and gentle woman, with long blonde hair that flowed down her back and a dress that reached her ankles. Berenice often cooked delicious meals for her family, kept the house tidy, and knew how to make clothes, candles, and soap from the things she found on the island. She was smart and creative, and she told her children stories and sang them songs.

Pieter, the oldest child, was ten years old, and looked like his father, with curly brown hair that bounced on his shoulders and a shirt that kind of matched his eyes. Pieter wanted to learn everything he could about the island and the world. He was curious and eager, and, when not in school, helped his father with the farm work and looked after his younger siblings. He loved his family very much, and he always listened to them when they spoke. Then, there was Anna, the middle child who was eight and looked like her mother. Anna had straight blonde hair that shone in the sun, a skirt that swirled around her legs, and loved animals and flowers; the girl was gentle and shy. Anna shared her toys and treats with her brothers and friends.

Willem, the youngest, was six, with spiky red hair that stood up on his head and shorts that showed his knees. The little man liked to run around; playing pranks was his favourite pastime, and he had a lot of fun with it. He was lively and mischievous, and he followed his father on his hunting trips and explored the island with his dog.

The family loved their life on the island; enjoying the sunshine, the breeze, and the fruits, and even had many friends among both the other settlers and the native people. They were happy and prosperous, but they also had a problem: they had become bored with eating the same things every day: bread, cheese, eggs, milk, and meat from the farm. And even though they tried to spice up their meals with some local herbs and sauces, they still felt something was missing. Oh, how the family craved something different and exciting, something that would tickle their taste buds and make them feel alive. Like all other settlers on this beautiful place, they had heard of a wonderful bird that lived on the island, a bird that was unlike any other bird they had ever seen; everyone called this bird the dodo, a ratite that wasn't afraid of humans. The family heard that out of curiosity, the dodo actually would approach the visitors who came to the island. They also heard that the dodo meat was tough and tasteless; but Mr and Mrs De Groot did not believe that and thought that the meat must be special and delicious and that it would be a treat; a delicacy. They wanted to try it and to find out for themselves what kind of meat it was. They wanted to have it for dinner – someday. But the dodo was difficult to find, as by this time in its history, it had become rare and elusive; living in the remote and dense forests of the island. Now that there were just a few of them left, it was becoming obvious that soon the dodo might go into extinction, but Mr and Mrs De Groot only cared about their hunger and their Dodo fillet curiosity.

One day, Jansen went on a hunt for the dodo. He said to his wife and children, "I'm going to the forest to look for something else to eat. I'll be back before sunset." Berenice kissed her husband goodbye and said, "Be careful, my dear. Don't go too far. Don't take any risks. Come back soon." He then took his gun, his knife, and his dog, and set off into the forest. He waved to his family and disappeared into the trees. She went back to the house and started to prepare the vegetables and the bread for dinner. She said to her children, "Come on, kids. Let's do our chores. Pieter, fetch some water from the well and some eggs from the chicken coop. Anna, go wash the dishes and set the table. Willem, sweep the floor and feed the cat. Do your chores quickly and quietly, and don't make any trouble." The children obeyed their mother, and worked hard and fast, hoping to finish soon and have some fun.

But Willem was not very good at sweeping. The boy missed some spots and made some dust because he got distracted after seeing a butterfly and chasing it and forgot about his chores and his mother's instructions. Berenice noticed that Willem was not sweeping when she looked out of the window and saw him playing with the insect. She was not happy and so called out to him and said, "Willem, what are you doing? Come back here and finish your work. You're being naughty and lazy." Willem heard his mother and felt guilty. The boy quickly dropped the butterfly and ran back to the house. "I'm sorry, mother. I won't do it again." Berenice accepted his apology and smiled. "It's all right, Willem. You're forgiven. But you have to be good. You can play after you're done. You're a good boy and I love you."

Meanwhile, Mr Jansen De Groot was having a hard time finding any Dodo. He walked through the forest and looked for any signs of the bird. Of course, there were some tracks and droppings, but he did not see any Dodo and wondered where all the birds had gone; thinking maybe they had sensed his presence and hidden, or perhaps they had been scared by the pirates.

Jansen was about to give up and go back home when he heard a strange and loud noise. It sounded like a mix of a honk and a croak, and it came from behind a bush, so he hurried to the bush and pushed it aside. There, the man saw a large, older-looking dodo sitting on the ground and looking at him with its round, innocent eyes. This was the last dodo on the island, and it did not know that it was in danger. That was why the dodo did not even try to run or hide, but just stayed there and waited for him to come closer.

The farmer could not believe it. He had found the dodo, and it was right in front of him and he knew what he had to do. With the greatest excitement, Mr Jansen De Groot simply raised the gun and aimed before pulling the trigger. The dodo fell backwards, collapsed to the ground, and passed away. But unbeknownst to Jansen, he had just murdered the last dodo in the world!

The farmer picked up the bird and put it on the horse, took off, and rode back to the farm where his anxious wife was waiting for his return before making DINNER.......!

Now, there were no more dodos left in existence. They all disappeared from the world and became extinct. Dodo the last died in 1662; he never saw Nakike again!!

13: DODO'S LEGACY

Dodo was special and left a lasting impact on the conscience of the whole world. His extinction was a tragic event that taught us a lot about the consequences of our actions on the environment. His story also inspires us to make efforts to save the dodo and its ecosystem and to protect other endangered species. Other living beings that depended on it felt the consequences of the dodo's extinction. One of them was the calvaria tree, which was the favourite food of the dodo. The calvaria tree had a hard shell that only the dodo could crack open with its big beak. The dodo also helped to spread the seeds of the tree around the island by pooping them out after eating the fruits. Without the dodo, the calvaria tree could not reproduce and grow more trees. Deforestation and invasive species also threatened the calvaria tree, and it became very rare and endangered.

Another consequence of the dodo's extinction was the loss of biodiversity and ecological balance on the island of Mauritius. The dodo was part of a complex web of life that included many other animals and plants. The dodo played a role in maintaining the health and diversity of the island's ecosystem by eating and dispersing seeds, pollinating flowers, and providing food and shelter for other creatures. Without the dodo, the island's ecosystem became less stable and resilient, and more vulnerable to disturbances and negative changes.

Dodo's extinction also had a cultural and historical impact on the world, as the special bird became a symbol of the effects of human activities on nature, and a reminder of the importance of conservation and respect for all living beings. The dodo also became a source of fascination and curiosity for many people who wanted to learn more about the bird and its history. The ratite also inspired many artists and writers who used the bird as a character or a theme in their works; that was one of the reasons that this book came to be written.

The dodo's extinction has now motivated us to make efforts to save the dodo and its ecosystem and to protect other endangered species. Some of these efforts were:

Colossal Biosciences, a biotech company that aimed to 'de-extinct' the dodo by using gene editing and stem cell technologies, launched the dodo Restoration Project in 2023; using the Nicobar pigeon, the closest living relative of the dodo, as a surrogate, to create a hybrid lineage that resembled the dodo. The project also planned to restore the dodo's habitat in Mauritius by planting calvaria trees and removing invasive species. The project faced many challenges and criticisms, and many scientists and conservationists questioned its feasibility and ethics.

A group of scientists, historians, and enthusiasts who wanted to preserve the memory and legacy of the dodo found the dodo Conservation Trust in 2022. Members of the trust collected and studied the remains and artefacts of the dodo, such as bones, feathers, paintings, and writings; they also created a museum and a website dedicated to the dodo, where people could learn more about the bird and its history. The trust also supported the conservation and restoration of the dodo's habitat and the calvaria tree in Mauritius. The United Nations established the dodo Awareness Day in 2021 as an annual event to raise awareness and education about the dodo and its extinction. They celebrated the day on 24 September, the date of the last confirmed sighting of the dodo in 1662. Celebrations featured various activities and events, such as exhibitions, lectures, workshops, quizzes, and games, that aimed to inform and inspire people about the dodo and its story. The day also encouraged people to take action and support the conservation and protection of other endangered species.

Dodo was a very special bird that left a lasting impact on the world. His extinction was a tragic event that taught us a lot about the consequences of our actions on the environment. His story also inspired us to make efforts to save the dodo and its ecosystem and to protect other endangered species. He was a very special bird, and, although he became extinct, lives on in our memories.

14: AT LAST – DODO RETURNS

Everything that has happened so far took place in the dreams of the geneticist. But the dream was now over, and the man had awakened from his slumber to face the realities that surrounded him. Nakike was now a very sad and lonely designer after realising that he had actually lost his best friend, Dodo, the bird that he had designed and given life to. Nakike didn't just lose him in the dream; he realised that he had also lost him in real life. The engineer remembered that in the dream, he had tried to save Dodo, but he was too late. He had never seen Dodo again, and he had never forgiven himself. Nakike missed him very much and wished he could see him again, hear his voice, and feel his feathers. He wished he could play with him just one more time; perhaps teach him new things and share his food with him. He wished he could bring him back to life and make him happy and healthy again.

A very long time passed, but one day, Nakike had an idea. The engineer remembered every detail of what happened in his Dodo dream; this made him conclude that he could bring the original program and prototype that he had used to create Dodo to reality. He wondered if he could use them to recreate Dodo and bring him back to life. He decided to try it, and he hoped it would work.

Nakike went to his real laboratory, where he had his computer and his machines. Using the program and prototype that he remembered, he built a robotic system and an incubator and checked them carefully to make sure they would work well, making some adjustments and improvements. From there, Nakike designed a dodo model and added new genes and features to it, to make him more resilient. He also added some memories and emotions to Dodo, to make him more aware of dangers. Nakike then used his machine to turn his prototype into an actual bird, but he did not want to use an egg; instead, he used a kind of scientific resurrection. His method was to use a special device that could scan the prototype and copy its genes and cells. He then used another device to assemble the genes and cells into the tissues of a living organism. All this required a lot of energy and time, and he was very patient as he waited while the computer vibrated and the incubator whined and rumbled.

Finally, after what seemed like an eternity, the machine beeped and opened. Inside, there was a bird that looked like a dodo and had a big beak, a fluffy body, and short legs. He also had bright eyes, a soft voice, and a warm heart. Dodo was alive, and he looked at Nakike with curiosity and recognition.

"Hello, Dodo. I'm Nakike, your creator and your friend. I'm so happy to see you again."

"Hello, Nakike," Dodo said."

Oh, Nakike was overjoyed! He had succeeded in recreating Dodo and bringing him back to life.

"Welcome back to the world, Dodo. This is your home. It's a laboratory where I work as a genetics designer. I make new animals like you in this place."

"Wow, that's amazing. What are animals?"

"Animals are living beings that have different shapes, sizes, and abilities. Some can fly, some can swim, some can run, and some can do other things. They are very diverse and wonderful."

"Can I fly?" Dodo asked.

"Yes, you can," Nakike said. "I made you a flying bird because I wanted you to be free and happy. You can fly, because you have wings and feathers. You can fly because you have dreams and hopes. Flying would also allow you to escape from danger, meaning you'll never be extinct again...!"

"Thank you, Nakike," Dodo said. "You are generous. You made me a wonderful bird, and I'm delighted and grateful."

"You're welcome; really. You know...., No Dodo is an island; that's why I am so happy to bring you back......, It's because I love you!"

Nakike hugged Dodo and felt a warm feeling in his heart. He was very pleased and proud to see the wonderful bird he had designed. He felt a strong bond with him, and he knew they would be best friends – again. The friends had a great time together; they looked forward to more adventures, and they never felt lonely or bored ever again. The designer and Dodo loved each other very much, and together, they cared for and protected many of the earth's species. They were the best of friends, and they lived happily ever after.

The End!

INDEX OF DANDY AHURUONYE'S BOOKS 

DANDY AHURUONYE

The Whispering Poet

DODO RETURNS

Lifetime Stories from The Whispering Poet
dandyahuruonyebooks@gmail.com

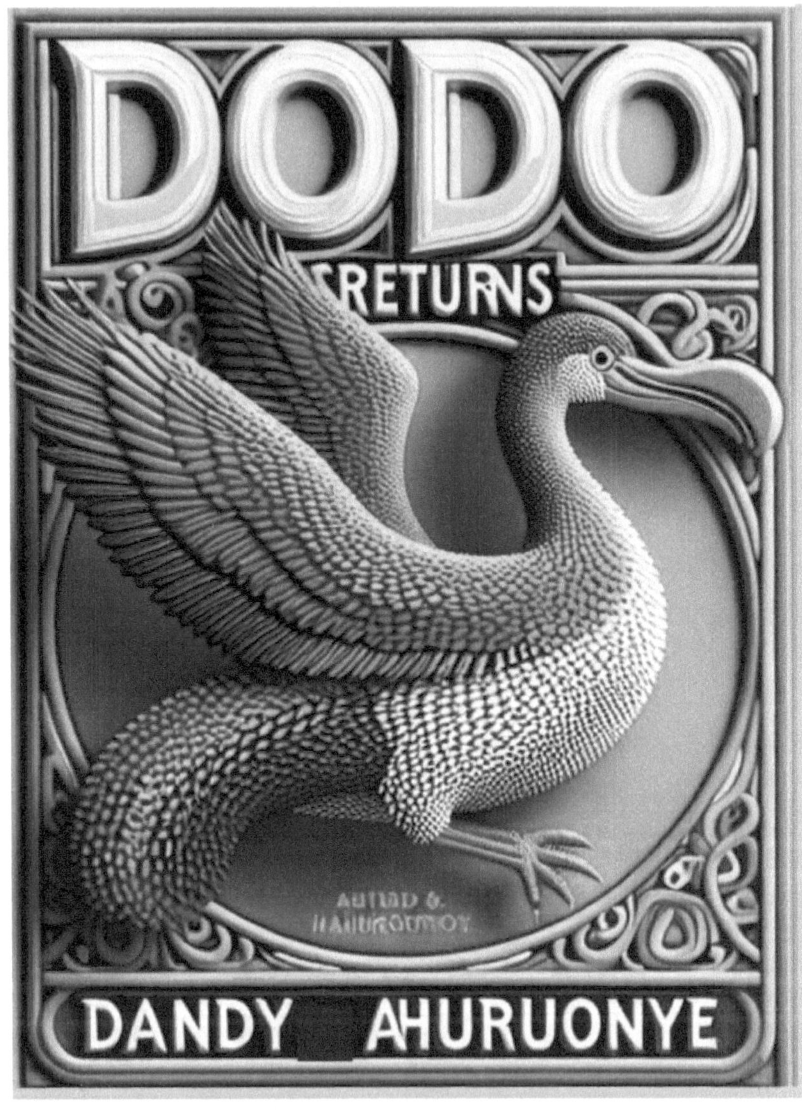
DODO
RETURNS
DANDY AHURUONYE

Don't miss out!

Visit the website below and you can sign up to receive emails whenever Dandy Ahuruonye publishes a new book. There's no charge and no obligation.

https://books2read.com/r/B-A-YNSQ-GHZSC

BOOKS 2 READ

Connecting independent readers to independent writers.

Also by Dandy Ahuruonye

THE WHISPERING POET: An Anthology of Igbo And Other
Proverbs
Grocc-ofly
Reading Glasses for Mama Eagle
The Cute Kids of Madugascar
Nora never gave up
A Fishhook and the Riverboy
Positive Brainwash
Groccolli
The Adventures of Groccolli
Happyville
Oh, What a Mars!
Stinky and The Dung Beetle
The Gull Who Must be Obeyed
THE SHOEMAKER: Principles & Guide for Professionals
The Groccolli Pictureland Chatbook
Finding Love in Cahersiveen
Trillion-Her
Lagos Teens and The Marketplace of Dreams
Why Did The Wasp Come?
Lower
Dodo Returns
Roosta & Henn: The Rise of AI Robots
The Eel, The Duck, and the Groccolli Ring of Love

Watch for more at https://wordpress.com/home/
dandyahuruonye.wordpress.com.

About the Author

Dandy Ahuruonye is the author of: 'Long Search for Greener Pastures,' and the technical manual on footwear designing: 'THE SHOEMAKER-Principles & Guide for Professionals;' 'DESIGNER'S FINGER: A Practical Guide For Shoe Professionals; 'The Grass Fart in Donegal Bay;' 'Waboubou;' 'Shokeleke;' 'Zinzie;' 'Metu;' 'Laka;' and 'THE WHISPERING POET: An Anthology of Igbo & Other Proverbs.'

Read more at https://dandyahuruonye.wordpress.com/.